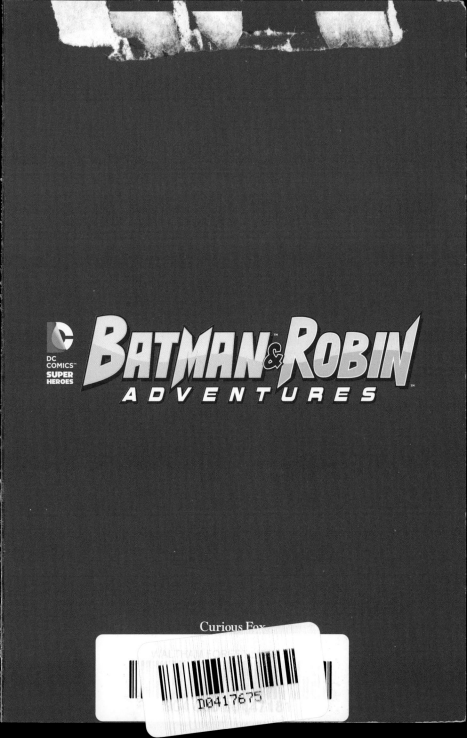

DC COMICS™
SUPER HEROES

BATMAN & ROBIN
ADVENTURES

Curious Fox

Published by Curious Fox,
an imprint of Capstone
Global Library Limited,
7 Pilgrim Street, London,
EC4V 6LB – Registered
company number: 6695582

www.curious-fox.com

STAR36548

The author's moral rights are hereby asserted.

ISBN 978 1 78202 353 1
20  19  18  17  16
10 9 8 7 6 5 4 3 2 1

A full catalogue for this book is available from the
British Library.

Editor: Christopher Harbo
Designer: Hilary Wacholz


Printed and bound in China.

DC COMICS SUPER HEROES

# BATMAN & ROBIN
## ADVENTURES

# TWO-FACE FACE-OFF

BY **LAURIE S. SUTTON**

ILLUSTRATED BY
**LUCIANO VECCHIO**

**BATMAN CREATED BY BOB KANE**

# CONTENTS

# CHAPTER 1

# FACE-TO-FACE

Batman and Robin raced towards the scene of danger. There was an escape happening at the Arkham Asylum for the Criminally Insane and they had to stop it!

"Who's trying to escape? The Joker? The Riddler?" Robin asked as he and Batman drove in the Batmobile.

"Someone much worse than those two criminals put together," Batman replied. "It's Two-Face!"

The Dynamic Duo zoomed through the streets of Gotham City. It was after midnight and no one was on the roads except a few slow delivery trucks. The Batmobile passed them as fast as a bat in flight.

Suddenly, red and blue lights flashed behind the duo's dark vehicle. A siren screamed. Batman glanced at the rearview monitor screen on the instrument panel.

"It's the Gotham City police," Batman said.

The police cars quickly caught up to the Batmobile – and then passed it at high speed. The vehicles accelerated down the street and ignored the Batmobile.

"I wonder where they're going in such a hurry," Robin said.

"That's no mystery," Batman replied. "Arkham."

"Attention, Batman and Robin!" a voice boomed over a loudspeaker. It came from another police vehicle that drove up behind the Batmobile.

"I recognize that voice. It's Police Commissioner Gordon," Batman said.

The Dark Knight pressed a button on the instrument panel of the Batmobile. It opened a radio communication channel between the two cars.

"Let's keep our conversation quiet," Batman said to the commissioner. "I wouldn't want to violate any late-night noise regulations."

"I see you're on your way to Arkham Asylum," Gordon said. "We need to get there fast. Follow our squad cars. We'll give you a police escort."

The police vehicle's engine roared as it passed the Batmobile and sped down the dark city street. Its warning lights flashed and its siren wailed. The Dark Knight's foot barely touched the accelerator pedal to catch up with the commissioner's car. The Batmobile moved silently through the night.

It didn't take long for Batman and Robin to arrive at the scene. As they approached, they could see it was chaos. The flashing lights of police vehicles filled the night with red and blue brilliance. A pair of police helicopters hovered above the asylum and pierced the dark with bright searchlights.

The Batmobile halted in front of a line of police officers and squad cars. The GCPD formed a perimeter like an army prepared to wage battle. Police radios squawked. Protective armour and shields were deployed.

Commissioner Gordon jumped out of his vehicle and took control like a general. Batman and Robin got out of the Batmobile and quietly headed for the shadows.

The Dynamic Duo avoided the bright spotlights from the police helicopters and found an area of deep darkness near the tall stone wall of the asylum. They each used hand-held launchers to fire a pair of grapnels over the wall towards the roof of the asylum building. They could not see exactly where the grapnels landed, but the sound of a solid **CLINK!** let them know that the hooks were secure.

Batman pressed a lever on his launcher and the Batrope attached to the grapnel pulled him up and over the wall. Robin activated the lever on his launcher and followed his partner into the asylum.

Robin landed on the roof tiles of Arkham and almost slipped on the moss growing there. His boots scuffed the green growth, which released a stinky stench. Robin forced himself to hold back a coughing fit. It was important to be very quiet. Stealth was a basic part of the Dynamic Duo's crime-fighting method.

The building was old and there were many odd quirks to its architecture. Robin hurried to follow Batman over the peaks and valleys of the roof. He could barely see the shadowy outline of the Dark Knight even with all the police lights.

Suddenly Batman dropped out of Robin's view. Robin almost let out a gasp of surprise. He rushed over the slippery roof tiles to the spot where Batman disappeared.

Light from an open skylight beamed up into Robin's face. There was a hallway below, and Robin caught sight of the end of Batman's cape whipping down the corridor.

The bright lights inside Arkham Asylum hurt Robin's eyes when he dropped down from the dark roof. That didn't stop him from following his partner into peril. Robin ran down the corridor.

The sound of fighting reached Robin moments before the sight of it did. **POW! WHAM! THUD!** Then he saw it – Batman battling Two-Face!

One half of the criminal's face was a permanent snarl. His lips were pulled back and one eye bulged from its socket. The other half of his face was handsome. Two-Face was split down the middle, fifty-fifty.

Two-Face pushed a hospital trolley towards Batman. It still had a patient strapped to it. The Dark Knight caught the trolley and shoved it aside. The patient laughed like a hyena.

Robin tried to run faster, but the slime on his boots made it difficult for him to get a grip on the floor. He couldn't speed up. Then he remembered Batman telling him: *always look for a way to turn a disadvantage into an advantage.* Robin realized that the slick moss on his boots could be an advantage after all.

Robin used the slime on his boots to slide across the floor. He stretched out his arms for balance and leaned forward for more speed. Robin aimed himself at Two-Face.

Robin hit his target. ***POW!*** Two-Face slammed into the wall and then tumbled to the floor. He did not get up.

Batman walked over to his junior partner and helped him to his feet.

"Nice work," the Dark Knight said.

"Thanks," Robin replied. He looked at the limp body of Two-Face. "What did he hope to gain by trying to escape?"

"The coin ... the coin," Two-Face moaned as he lay curled on the floor.

"The coin is in the vault, Harvey," a voice said. It belonged to a woman in a white doctor's coat. "You don't need the coin, Harvey. It doesn't control you."

Batman knew that Two-Face was once Harvey Dent, the district attorney for Gotham City. A vengeful attack had scarred Harvey both physically and mentally. Harvey used to represent the law. Now, as Two-Face, he led a life of crime.

"Dr Andrea Wye," Batman said. He read the woman's name on her ID tag. "You're new to Harvey's case."

"I'm trying a new therapy," Dr Wye said. "I'm hoping to get Harvey to give up his obsession with the double-faced coin. If he can't do that, he'll never be free."

"I must have my coin!" Two-Face shouted. He jumped to his feet with a tremendous burst of energy. He shoved Dr Wye into Robin and they fell against the wall. **THUMP! CRASH!** They stumbled into the patient strapped to the hospital trolley. It twisted down the corridor like a spinning top.

"Heehee hahaha!" the patient cackled wildly.

"I must get my coin," Two-Face said as he ran down the corridor.

Batman deduced that Two-Face would head for the vault. He knew that Two-Face would not let anything stand between him and his precious double-faced coin. It had been with Two-Face ever since he had been scarred. It was just like him: one side looked normal, and the other side was etched with deep scratches. Defaced.

"I have to capture Two-Face before innocent people get hurt," Batman said and raced after his adversary.

The Dark Knight headed for the asylum vault in the basement level of the building. The vault contained the possessions of the super-villains in Arkham. It held the Joker's deadly joy buzzer and poison lapel flower, plus the Mad Hatter's hypnotic hats. Even more dangerous items like vials of Scarecrow's fear gas and Bane's venom were kept there.

Batman did not want Two-Face to get his hands on any of these things. A tremendous **BOOM!** from deep below told Batman he was too late!

Smoke churned out of the open vault door. Two GCPD guards staggered towards the Dark Knight.

"We tried to stop him," Officer Jensen said.

"We think he's still in there," Officer Abbey added.

"Good," Batman replied as he pulled a breathing mask from his Utility Belt and ran straight into the blinding cloud.

Night-vision lenses in his cowl let Batman see the shape of Two-Face searching the shelves. Suddenly the villain held up a shiny object in triumph.

"My coin!" Two-Face declared.

Batman threw a Batarang attached to a Batrope and lassoed his adversary. Two-Face struggled to break free of the rope and smashed into the giant shelves. They started to tumble. **CRASH! BOOM! SMASH!** One of the heavy shelves knocked the Dark Knight out of the vault.

Batman was a trained athlete and acrobat. He used his skills to roll along the floor and then spring back onto his feet. He returned to the vault, but when he got inside, Two-Face was gone. So was the double-faced coin.

# CHAPTER 2
## FASHION FRENZY

"It's been days since Two-Face escaped from Arkham Asylum," Robin said. "He should have done something by now. What's he waiting for?"

"Two-Face could make his move in the next two hours, or in two weeks. He always works in twos," Batman replied.

"It's been too long," Robin grumbled as he tapped a button on the keyboard in front of him.

The Dynamic Duo monitored the police reports and news feeds from the Batcomputer in the Batcave. Suddenly a large red dot appeared on the monitor screen. A text window popped up to describe the activity being reported.

**ROBBERY IN PROGRESS**

**ART INSTITUTE OF GOTHAM CITY**

**INCIDENT WARNINGS: UNREPORTED**

"Hmmm," Batman said. "Bruce Wayne received an invitation for a charity event at the Art Institute. It was for a fashion show."

The Dark Knight led two lives. One as Bruce Wayne, billionaire businessman. The other as Batman, defender of Gotham City.

"Can't the police take care of a robbery at a fashion show?" Robin asked. "We need to find Two-Face."

"We've found him. The House of Deux sent the invitation. 'Deux' means 'two' in French. The designers are twin sisters," Batman said.

Robin did an information search on the Batcomputer. Several news articles about the show popped up on the screen. He scanned the stories to glean as much information as he could.

"Not only that, the designers are using rare twin diamonds called the Gemini Gems as part of the show," Robin said.

"Gemini is the Zodiac symbol of the twins," Batman said.

"More twos," Robin realized.

"That's too much for Two-Face to resist," Batman said. "Let's see how he deals with the Dynamic Duo."

Batman and Robin ran to the Batmobile. They jumped into their seats and the automatic safety harnesses wrapped around them. The engine came to life. A string of lights lit up an exit tunnel. Batman stomped on the accelerator.

The powerful vehicle shot down the underground tunnel like a rocket being launched. The Batmobile zoomed out of a camouflaged exit and headed towards Gotham City.

Batman tuned into the GCPD's radio channel and listened to the chatter between the officers who surrounded the Art Institute. He could hear Commissioner Gordon's voice directing his men.

"It sounds like Gordon is forming a perimeter on street level," Batman said. "You and I will go in from above."

The Dark Knight stopped the Batmobile a few blocks away from the Art Institute. He got out of the vehicle and launched a Batrope into the night sky. **CLINK!** The grapnel attached to it caught on the window ledge near the top of a building. **ZIP!** Up he went. Robin followed. The Dynamic Duo used the rooftops instead of the streets to arrive at the Art Institute.

They entered the building from the roof. The lock on the maintenance door was designed to keep out thieves. It was not a barrier for the electronic lock-picking device in Batman's Utility Belt.

The Dynamic Duo entered the building and ran down the stairs to the gallery level where the fashion show was taking place. There, they paused and observed Two-Face as he robbed the guests.

The villain had a gang of henchmen doing the dirty work. They went among the partygoers and took their jewellery. Two-Face stood in the middle of the room with the Gemini Gems in his hands.

"We'll split up and come at Two-Face from two directions," Batman whispered. Robin nodded and moved away silently.

A few moments later there were two sounds: **BANG! CLINK!** They were followed by two more: **BANG! CLINK!** A pair of grapnels gripped the ceiling of the gallery. Batman and Robin swooped down on Batropes.

Robin knocked down two of the henchmen with his boot heels. The men stumbled backwards and slammed into two other crooks. The bags of stolen jewellery tumbled from their hands.

Batman snatched the Gemini Gems out of Two-Face's hands and swung to the far side of the gallery. He dropped the gems down to the two fashion designers. Then he swung back towards Two-Face before the villain knew what was happening. **POW!** Batman let go of the Batrope and tackled Two-Face.

The criminal and the crime fighter slid on the polished marble floor. The partygoers couldn't move out of the way in time. They fell like bowling pins when Batman and Two-Face rolled into them. The impact let the villain wriggle out of Batman's grip.

Two-Face stood up and brushed off his black-and-white suit. He acted confident as Batman struggled to get out from under the partygoers on top of him. Out of the corner of his eye, Batman saw Robin get ready to throw a Batarang. Two-Face saw Robin, too.

"Stop right now or all of these people could get hurt!" Two-Face said. He reached into the pocket of his jacket and pulled out a fake flower.

Batman froze. He recognized the flower. The Dark Knight shook his head ever so slightly in a silent message to Robin. *Don't move.*

"I see that you took more than just your coin from the vault at Arkham Asylum," Batman said.

"Yes, I did," Two-Face replied. He pinned the fake flower onto the black lapel of his suit. "It's a bit gaudy, but it belongs to the Joker, after all."

"That's the Joker's poison lapel flower!" Robin blurted. He regretted his hasty words instantly.

The crowd of partygoers gasped in fear. They murmured among themselves. Someone started to cry.

"I see that these people know the power of this flower," Two-Face said. He turned around in a circle so that everyone in the room could see it. "Should I use that power ... or not?"

Two-Face reached into another pocket and pulled out his double-faced coin. He held it in front of his face.

"The flower is loaded with Joker Venom. Do I use it on these people, or do I let them live? They have a fifty-fifty chance, Batman," Two-Face said. "If the coin lands with the scarred side up, I release the toxin. If it lands with the undamaged side showing, they are safe."

Two-Face threw the coin into the air.

The people did not give the Dark Knight a chance to answer. They did not wait to see if the coin landed with the scarred side up or down. They all started to run. The people on top of Batman scrambled to their feet and fled. This freed the Dark Knight to take action!

The coin flipped and tumbled in the air. Two-Face watched it intensely. He did not take his eyes off it as it spun over and over in mid-air. **SHHHKIIIING!** Suddenly a Batarang struck the coin and knocked it across the gallery. It disappeared beneath the feet of the stampeding partygoers.

"Noooo!" Two-Face yelled. "My coin! I must have my coin!"

Batman ran forward and tackled his distracted enemy.

"Robin! Get the coin while I take down Two-Face," the Dark Knight instructed his junior partner.

Batman snatched the Joker's poison flower off Two-Face's lapel and threw it out of the criminal's reach. Two-Face threw a punch at Batman, but the Dark Knight ducked his head to one side. Batman grabbed Two-Face's outstretched fist.

**CLICK!** He snapped a Bat-cuff onto the criminal's wrist.

"I'm taking you back to Arkham," the Dark Knight told Two-Face.

"I'm not going back there," Two-Face said. "The food is terrible."

"I found the coin, Batman!" Robin shouted from across the gallery. He held it up in the air for Batman to see.

Two-Face was filled with fear and anger when he saw his precious coin in the hands of his enemy. He thought of the coin as a part of himself. It was a part of his identity. He could not be separated from it.

A sudden burst of desperation surged through Two-Face. He shoved Batman and the Dark Knight fell backwards. Two-Face ran towards Robin. Along the way, he grabbed the Joker's poison flower from the floor. Two-Face pointed it at Robin.

"Give me the coin, kid, or I'll gas you," the villain said.

"Okay, okay," Robin said as he held up his hands in surrender. "Here. Catch."

Robin threw the coin towards Two-Face. The criminal watched it soar over his head and towards Batman.

"Double-crosser," Two-Face growled.

"Surrender, Two-Face," Batman said as he caught the coin.

"I have a second option," Two-Face said as he grabbed Robin and held the Joker flower in front of his face. "You give me the coin and the Boy Wonder lives to fight crime another day."

"How do I know you won't gas him even if I give you the coin?" Batman asked.

"You don't. But I have a good side, too, remember?" Two-Face replied. "That's what the coin decides."

The Dark Knight looked down at the coin in his hand. The undamaged side represented the good side of Two-Face that had once been Harvey Dent. The scarred side of the coin reflected the twisted personality that drove him to commit crime.

"Let's let the coin decide," Batman said.

The Dark Knight flipped the coin with his thumb, but it did not go straight up into the air. It flew towards the gallery door. The police waited outside that door.

Two-Face let go of Robin and raced to retrieve his coin before it – and he – ended up in the hands of the GCPD.

Robin's shoulders slumped. "You let him go because of me," he said. "I failed you."

"Two-Face didn't get the Gemini Gems or hurt any of the partygoers. I'd say that was a success, not a failure," Batman replied. "Don't worry, we'll get a second chance to capture Two-Face."

# CHAPTER 3
# COIN CRIME

Bruce Wayne walked up the stone steps outside the Gotham City Exhibition Centre. He was dressed in a tuxedo to attend a charity event. Bruce was one of Gotham City's most prominent citizens. He was always getting invitations to fund-raisers.

But this fund-raiser was different. The main attraction was a set of rare twin coins. It was a prize that would attract Two-Face. Bruce was not going to ignore this party the way he had ignored the fashion show.

"I can't see any sign of Two-Face so far," Robin said through the tiny two-way radio in Bruce Wayne's ear. "Do you really think he's going to crash this party?"

"Yes. The highlight of the charity auction is a matching pair of unique gold coins called Double Eagles. They're proofs struck by the US Mint in 1849 and only two of them exist in the whole world. Two-Face won't be able to resist," Bruce whispered.

"Well, I'm in my 'Robin's nest' above the Exhibition Centre. I'll be able to see Two-Face if he shows up anywhere within a six-block radius," Robin said to his partner.

"There's a fifty-fifty chance that he might use an underground route to get inside. That's why you're the eyes in the sky and I'm the eyes on the ground," Bruce replied.

"First one to spot Two-Face gets to drive the Batmobile for a week," Robin challenged.

Bruce smiled but did not respond. He stepped through the doors of the Exhibition Centre. He handed his party invitation to a woman dressed in a sparkly gown. She smiled at him without even looking at the invitation card. She knew who he was. All the women in Gotham City knew who he was. He was a billionaire bachelor.

"Good evening, Mr Wayne! Welcome!" the woman said enthusiastically. "I see that you don't have a date tonight."

"A date? No, but I expect to have a business partner join me in a little while," Bruce replied and walked past her into the main hall. The room was huge. It was used for large events like conventions and car shows.

Tonight it was filled with glamorous people and giant prop coins. The centre-piece was a pair of replica Double Eagle coins three metres in diameter. The real coins were in a display case in front of them.

Bruce walked over to the display for a closer look at the security in place. A pair of GCPD officers stood guard. Bruce looked at the names on their badges.

"Good evening, Officer Jensen, Officer Abbey," Bruce greeted them politely. He remembered seeing them guarding the vault at Arkham.

"Mr Wayne," the officers replied. One of them looked him over as if searching for a hidden weapon. The other never took his eyes off the crowd. The crime fighter in Bruce appreciated their tactics. It showed the tight teamwork between the two partners.

Bruce glanced around the hall to analyze his surroundings. He noticed the metal catwalks hanging from the high ceiling. *Those are excellent for anchoring a grapnel, and high enough to swing from a Batrope,* he thought. He saw large air-conditioning vents. *Two-Face could get into the hall from any one of those.*

Suddenly his thoughts were interrupted by a loud **BAAANG!** All the lights in the hall went out. The GCPD guards pulled their torches and Tasers and held them in front of their bodies defensively. One of the officers grabbed Bruce by his sleeve.

"Get behind me, Mr Wayne," she said.

Bruce stepped back a few paces. He stood between the display case and the giant replica coins.

"Two-Face must be responsible for this," Bruce whispered into his two-way radio to Robin. "The lights and alarms are out. Get down here, now."

"I'm on my way," Robin replied.

Under the cover of darkness, Bruce Wayne turned to the secret spot at the Exhibition Centre where he had stashed a spare Batsuit earlier in the day. He switched into his costume and wasted no time activating the night-vision lenses in his cowl.

The lenses enhanced the light the GCPD guards' torches cast throughout the hall. They made the people in the hall look like eerie green ghosts. Batman watched them run around in a panic. He expected to see that. Then he saw a small group walking calmly towards the giant coin display. That was not normal.

"Ah, there you are, Two-Face," Batman said to himself. He could clearly see the outline of the criminal and his henchmen. "And it looks like you've brought some pals with you."

The Dark Knight looked up at the metal struts of the catwalks above him. Batman launched a grapnel towards the ceiling. **CLAAANG!** It gripped the metal struts and Batman used the Batrope attached to it to swing towards Two-Face.

It was easy to find his target even without the night-vision lenses. Two-Face and his gang stood in the spotlight of a pair of torch beams. The GCPD guards held their ground and defended the precious Double Eagle coins in the display case.

Suddenly a large, dark shape landed between the two brave officers.

"Batman!" one of the guards gasped in surprise.

"Batman!" Two-Face growled.

Another costumed crime fighter dropped from a Batrope and landed next to the Dark Knight. "Hey, don't forget me!"

"Robin!" the second guard exclaimed.

"It looks like you saw Two-Face first, Batman. You get to drive the Batmobile for a week," Robin said.

**KSHUNK!** The sound of the emergency generators starting was followed by the dull glow of the back up lights. **BRIIING! BRIIING!** Alarm bells started to ring. Partygoers rushed for the exit doors. Batman and Robin and the two police officers stood like a human wall between Two-Face and the Double Eagle coins.

Two-Face continued to walk at a casual pace towards the four defenders. On the outside he looked calm, but on the inside he was very angry. He wanted those golden coins!

Two-Face flipped his double-faced coin up and down as if trying to decide what to do. Batman made the decision for him. **ZWOOSH!** A Batarang sped through the air. It missed hitting Two-Face's double-faced coin by an inch. Two-Face grabbed his coin out of the air and tightened his fist around the precious object.

"That's the second time you've tried that trick, only this time it didn't work," Two-Face said with a sneer.

"Then how about this trick?" Robin said as he grabbed a police-issue Taser from one of the guards and fired.

The double wires uncoiled as they raced towards Two-Face. Without a second thought, Two-Face threw one of his henchmen into the path of the stun device.

"Urrrk!" The bad guy flopped on the floor.

"One down," Robin said. He pointed a finger at the rest of the henchmen as if counting them one by one. "Five to go."

"Get them!" Two-Face ordered his men.

The remaining henchmen raced towards the Dynamic Duo. Batman and Robin met the assault with Batarangs and martial arts training. Batman blocked a blow from one of the henchmen then grabbed his wrist. The Dark Knight used his opponent's forward motion to flip him onto his back. The impact knocked the breath from the man's lungs and the sense from his head.

Robin pulled a Batarang from his Utility Belt and threw it at his foe. The henchman dodged the device. It whizzed past him.

"Nice try, Boy Wonder," the henchman said, laughing at Robin's failed attempt. He stalked towards Robin with his hands out, ready to grab the young crime fighter. Robin did not move. He did not look afraid. He actually smiled.

"Wait for it," Robin said to his enemy.

The Batarang arched around and came back to knock out the henchman. **SMACK!** The bad guy went down like a bag of heavy bricks. Robin reached down and picked up the device.

"This Batarang is also a boomerang," Robin told his unconscious foe. "It always comes back."

While the crime fighters were busy battling his henchmen, Two-Face saw that the Double Eagle coins were unguarded. This was his chance to grab them. He reached out towards the display case. **ZWIIIIP!** The case lifted into the air and out of his reach. Two-Face gaped after it, surprised. Then he saw a Batrope wrapped around the case.

"Batman!" Two-Face grumbled.

The display case dangled like a piñata from a Batrope looped over the catwalk. Batman stood near by holding the other end of the rope in his hands.

Two-Face worried that he had lost the coins. He would lose his freedom next if he didn't do something. Two-Face shoved one of the giant prop coins with all his strength. It started to roll. The huge coin headed towards the partygoers who were crowding the exits.

"Choose, Batman! Let go of the rope so you can save those people, or hang onto it and watch innocent people get crushed," Two-Face said. He flipped his scarred coin. The scratched face landed upright.

"I'm not the one bound to the decision of the coin, Two-Face," the Dark Knight reminded his foe.

Batman ran towards the rolling coin while still holding the Batrope. The display case zoomed up even higher out of Two-Face's reach. Batman leaped onto the top of the giant prop and ran on its edge like a lumberjack on a rolling log. He guided the coin away from the frightened crowd.

"I've struck out twice, but the game isn't over yet, Batman," Two-Face said as he used the distraction to escape.

# CHAPTER 4

# DOUBLE TROUBLE

Batman and Robin sat in front of the Batcomputer and studied the images on the giant monitor. There were at least ten open windows that displayed information on things that might attract Two-Face. The Dynamic Duo was doing a little detective work.

"There's a jewellery gallery exhibiting rare black-and-white diamonds," Robin said. "Two-Face would be interested in opposites like that."

"That's a possibility," Batman agreed. "Here's something else – a screening of famous comedy duos: Abbott and Costello, Laurel and Hardy, Lucy and Ricky."

"Who?" Robin asked.

"Hmm. It seems there's a serious gap in your classic entertainment education," Batman said.

"Hey, here's something. An exhibition of paintings of famous couples at the Gotham City Museum of Art," Robin said. He enlarged the news article that announced the event.

Batman studied the information and the photos of the paintings. The art showed Anthony and Cleopatra, David and Goliath and Dr Jekyll and Mr Hyde.

"Two-Face won't be able to resist stealing a portrait of Jekyll and Hyde," Batman said.

"That looks like our strongest possibility so far," Robin said.

"Except for this one," Batman replied. He punched up a story on the computer display about a priceless statue on loan to the Gotham City History Museum. The photo with the article showed a statue of a mother wolf with two human children.

"I recognize that statue! It's Romulus and Remus – the mythological founders of Rome," Robin said.

"Yes. They were orphaned and a wolf adopted them," Batman replied. "They were twin brothers."

"And we know how Two-Face likes things that come in twos," Robin said.

"We have two very strong contenders for where Two-Face might strike," Batman said.

"How do we decide between locations?" Robin asked.

"We don't have to decide. We can be in two places at the same time," Batman replied. "The Dynamic Duo will split up."

"How do we choose who goes to the art exhibit and who stakes out the statue?" Robin asked.

"We could flip a coin," Batman said.

Suddenly the Batcomputer monitor displayed two flashing red dots. A pair of text windows popped up.

**ROBBERY IN PROGRESS**

**GOTHAM CITY MUSEUM OF ART**

**INCIDENT WARNINGS: TWO-FACE REPORTED ON SCENE**

**ROBBERY IN PROGRESS**

**GOTHAM CITY HISTORY MUSEUM**

**INCIDENT WARNINGS: TWO-FACE REPORTED ON SCENE**

"It looks like our deductions were right about which exhibits might attract Two-Face," Batman said.

Robin read both of the text windows and scratched his head in confusion.

"How can those incident warnings be right?" Robin asked. "Two-Face can't be in two places at once."

"It can only mean that Two-Face has a doppelganger," Batman said. "A *double*."

"So one of them is a fake," Robin said. "But how do we know which is which?"

"We stick to our original plan to split up," Batman replied. "I'll go to the History Museum and you'll respond to the alert at the Museum of Art."

"Can I drive the Batmobile?" Robin asked hopefully.

"Not this time," Batman said. "The Redbird is fast enough."

Robin was disappointed, but only a little bit. Riding his specially designed motorcycle wasn't all bad. It could move through traffic better than the large Batmobile.

The Dynamic Duo ran to their vehicles. Batman jumped into the Batmobile and the safety harness clamped down over his chest. He pressed the ignition button and the sleek black car roared to life. **VROOOOM!** The vehicle was not in "quiet" mode as Batman zoomed down the tunnel.

Robin leaped onto his streamlined motorcycle and strapped a helmet onto his head. The visor's heads-up display lit up. He pressed the Redbird's starter button and the engine rumbled powerfully. Robin accelerated after the Batmobile. Together the Dynamic Duo headed out of the Batcave and towards Gotham City.

As soon as Batman and Robin crossed over the Gotham Bridge and entered Gotham City, Batman headed north and Robin headed south. The History Museum and the Museum of Art were at opposite ends of the city. That did not surprise the Dark Knight. Opposites were typical of Two-Face. But it did make Batman suspicious. If it was a strategy to keep the two crime fighters far apart, it was a good one.

This thought was on Batman's mind as he continued towards his destination. When he arrived at the Gotham City History Museum he saw that the GCPD was already there in great numbers. A perimeter of squad cars surrounded the building. Their lights flashed and the sounds of radio chatter filled the air.

Batman observed that no attempt had been made to enter the museum. He wondered why the police had not made a move. The Dark Knight worried that there were hostages inside. The police would not take action if civilians were threatened. Batman decided to find out for himself.

The Dark Knight entered the building through a service door. The door was locked, but it was a WayneTech lock. Batman knew the master security code.

Once inside the museum, it wasn't hard for Batman to find Two-Face. He was in the main exhibition hall where the statue of Romulus and Remus was on display. The criminal stood near by and flipped his coin, trying to decide what to do with the hostages at his feet. Two henchmen struggled to break into the shatterproof glass display case.

"Another set of henchmen?" Batman said out loud. "You seem to have an endless supply. Is there a Henchmen-For-Hire Agency I don't know about?"

Two-Face turned at the sound of the Dark Knight's voice. He did not seem surprised to see the crime fighter.

"I like to think I'm helping keep the unemployment rate down," Two-Face replied. He walked away from the hostages as if he didn't care about them.

"Well, I'm about to put you out of business," Batman said as he launched a Batarang at the crooks.

The Batarang hit one of the henchmen. It wasn't a very hard blow, but it was enough to knock the bad guy off balance. He fell into his pal and the two men tumbled away from the display case. No sooner did Batman release the Batarang than he pulled a small sphere from his Utility Belt and threw it at Two-Face. **FWOOOOSH!** A cloud of knockout gas erupted from the sphere.

"It's time for you and your pals to take a nap," the Dark Knight said.

When the gas dispersed, Batman expected to see Two-Face and his henchmen asleep on the floor. Instead, Two-Face stood as if nothing had happened. He flipped his coin up and down.

"Nose plugs," Two-Face revealed as he tapped the side of his nose. "And, I held my breath."

"Okay, then we do this the hard way," Batman said as he leaped towards the criminal.

The Dark Knight used his strength and acrobatic skills to jump from a standstill towards Two-Face and tackle him. *POW!* The villain went down under Batman's weight and skidded across the floor. The double-faced coin tumbled out of his hand and rolled out of his reach. Two-Face ignored it. He squirmed around in Batman's grip and tried to punch the Dark Knight.

Batman plunged his head to the side and dodged the sloppy assault. He grabbed Two-Face's wrist and quickly snapped a Bat-cuff on it. *CLICK!*

"I did this exact same thing at the House of Deux fashion show," Batman recalled. "It's not like Two-Face to make the same mistake twice."

Batman grabbed a flap of soft plastic hidden under the criminal's shirt collar and pulled. Two-Face's features wrinkled and bunched as the Dark Knight removed the man's mask.

"But you aren't the real Two-Face," Batman said. "I knew you were an imposter the moment you didn't chase after the coin."

The fake Two-Face glanced over to where the double-faced coin lay on the floor next to the hostages. The criminal shrugged.

"You were right when you said that Two-Face had an endless supply of henchmen," the criminal said. "He hires them from my agency!"

"And I was right that this was meant as a diversion all along," Batman said. "Two-Face wanted to divide the Dynamic Duo."

"Ha ha! It looks like the plan worked," the false Two-Face said.

As Batman freed the hostages, he spoke into the two-way radio that he and Robin used to communicate.

"Robin, come in. The Two-Face at the History Museum is the fake," Batman said. "The real Two-Face is at your location."

Batman waited to hear a reply from his partner. All he heard was silence.

"Robin, can you hear me?" Batman asked.

The voice that replied was one that the Dark Knight did not want to hear.

"Robin is ... not able to talk to you right now," Two-Face said.

"Harvey, don't hurt him. He's just a kid," Batman said, trying to reach the good side of Two-Face.

"I haven't decided what I'm going to do with him ... yet," Two-Face said.

Batman could hear the sound of the coin flipping in the air. Once. Twice. Three times.

"Two-Face, this is between the two of us. Leave Robin out of it," Batman said. "Let's meet. Tell me where to meet you."

There was another long silence as Two-Face hesitated, trying to play with Batman's nerves. But the Dark Knight was already racing from the museum.

"Meet me at Goodwin Airfield," Two-Face replied over the radio in Batman's ear. "I want to see if this robin can fly."

## CHAPTER 5
# THE FINAL FLIP

Robin woke up to total darkness. He felt groggy and his whole body was stiff. He could barely move his arms and legs. Slowly Robin realized that he felt stiff because he was tied up. It was dark because he was blindfolded.

"Two-Face," Robin murmured as he remembered battling the villain in the Museum of Art. "He knocked me out with some sort of gas."

Robin managed to work the blindfold up over his head. As soon as his eyes were uncovered he found himself eye-to-eye with a hideous face! A flash of light illuminated a glaring eye and scarred flesh.

For a second Robin thought Two-Face was leering at him. A moment later he realized it was the painting of Dr Jekyll and Mr Hyde that Two-Face had stolen from the museum.

Robin looked around and analyzed his surroundings. He was in a van. The only exit was a pair of doors at the back of the vehicle. There were a pair of windows set in the doors but they were either blacked out or very dirty.

"I don't know where Two-Face is taking me, but I don't plan on finding out," Robin said. "I'm getting out of here."

Robin twisted around on the floor of the vehicle and loosened the rope wrapped around his body. After a while he could move his elbows and then his arms. Robin wriggled like a worm until he could move his hands. His fingers found the knots that bound him.

The van stopped before Robin could complete his task. The engine turned off and Robin could hear the muffled voices of his abductors on the driver's side of the van. Then Robin heard the sounds of the front doors slamming and the tread of boots walking towards the back of the vehicle.

"Focus on the knots, not the bad guys," Robin said to himself as he worked to loosen his bonds. A section of rope released. Then another.

The back doors of the van opened. A pair of muscular henchmen stood in the doorway. One climbed into the back of the van. He saw a limp and unmoving prisoner.

"Aw, look. The poor little robin fainted with fright," the crook said.

The henchman grabbed Robin's ropes and started to drag him to the van doors. Suddenly the bad guy found himself holding an empty coil of rope.

"Huh? How did–?" the henchman started to say. He never finished.

Robin shoved the henchman against the inside of the van. **WHUMP!** The impact made a dent in the metal. The bad guy bounced back towards Robin and the Boy Wonder used the momentum to shove him against the opposite wall. The henchman fell to the floor and did not get up.

"Hey!" the second henchman yelled as he jumped into the back of the van.

It was a low and narrow space. Robin used the wall of the vehicle as a springboard to propel himself towards the bad guy. Robin scooted along the floor of the van and between the henchman's legs like a baseball player sliding into home. Robin zoomed through the back doors of the van. As soon as his feet hit the ground he turned and slammed the door shut on the furious bad guy. **CLICK!** Robin pressed the lock.

"You're good, kid," a voice said.

Robin didn't need to look to know who was speaking. He spun around and struck out at Two-Face with a kick. It didn't have to be accurate. It didn't even have to connect. It just needed to give Robin a few seconds to decide his next move.

Two-Face didn't give Robin those few seconds. The villain pointed a cylinder of knockout gas at his enemy. Robin knew it was the same stuff that had knocked him out at the Museum of Art. He jumped back to retreat – right into the grip of two bad guys.

"I always have two sets of henchmen," Two-Face said.

Robin didn't hesitate. He stomped on the foot of one of his captors. The bad guy bent over in pain. Robin used this motion to drag the man forward and flip him onto the ground. He broke his grip on Robin.

The second henchman was not expecting any resistance, so he was caught off balance by Robin's attack on his partner. In a single, smooth motion, Robin tripped the second henchman and dropped him to the pavement, too.

While Robin was distracted fighting the henchmen, Two-Face used the knockout gas on his foe. **HISSS!** The young crime fighter collapsed to the ground. Two-Face looked at Robin lying at his feet. Then he looked at his henchmen lying on the ground and those locked in the van.

"Why do I pay these people?" Two-Face said. "If a super-villain wants something done right, he has to do it himself."

* * *

When Robin woke up the second time, he knew he was in trouble before he even opened his eyes. He could feel the rush of a strong wind against his face and hear the low drone of an antique aeroplane motor. Robin lifted his eyelids and saw the sky all around him.

"I'm on an aeroplane," Robin realized. He looked around. "Actually, I'm on the wing of an aeroplane."

The young crime fighter discovered that he was on his back and tied to the top wing of a biplane. Suddenly the aircraft rolled upside down. Robin found himself facing the ground far below.

The ropes holding Robin to the wing stretched and groaned as his weight pulled against them. He saw a small airport and its single runway. A sleek black vehicle drove onto the runway and screeched to a halt.

"Batman," Robin said when he recognized the Batmobile.

The biplane flipped upright again and Robin heard a familiar voice shout over the sound of the engine.

"Batman!" Two-Face said from the open cockpit. "He's come to save his little robin."

The plane tipped on one wing and circled the airport. Robin could see the Batmobile, but there was no sign of the Dark Knight. Two-Face did not seem to notice. He was too wrapped up in proclaiming his mad threat.

"I'm going to flip my coin, Batman!" Two Face said over the radio Batman and Robin used to communicate. "If the scarred side comes up, I'm going to crash this biplane and Robin dies. I have a parachute. Your partner doesn't. If the clean side lands face-up, he lives. Which will it be?"

Two-Face threw the coin in the air. He was alarmed when the forward motion of the plane and the rushing wind from the propeller caught the surface of the coin and carried it backwards.

Two-Face barely caught his precious coin before it sailed out of his reach and fell to the ground far below. As soon as he had his coin safely in his hand, a streak of something large and black and fast zoomed past the biplane. Turbulence rocked the antique aircraft from side to side.

Robin felt the wing shudder under him. He used the vibration to help him loosen the ropes that held him. Just like in the van, once he got his fingers on the knots...

In the open cockpit of the biplane, Two-Face watched a black jet with bat-shaped wings head straight for him. He barely had time to realize what it was before the jet tipped a wing and flew in a spiral around the biplane. The antique aircraft lost its lift in the wake of unstable air created by the jet. It dropped towards the ground.

Two-Face tightened one hand around his precious coin and one hand on the strap of his parachute. He gripped the edge of the open cockpit, ready to jump. Suddenly a second person dropped into the cockpit.

"I suppose you don't have two of those?" Robin asked, looking at the villain's parachute. "How about we flip for it?"

Robin grabbed the controls of the biplane and sharply banked it upside down. Two-Face started to tumble out of the open cockpit. Robin reached out and pulled the ripcord of the villain's parachute. The chute deployed immediately. Two-Face drifted through the air, but never reached the ground.

**ZROOOMM!** The Batplane gripped Two-Face's parachute with a Bat-grapple. Batman banked the Batplane and flew the villain back to Arkham Asylum.

With Two-Face safely in custody, Robin landed the biplane at Goodwin Airfield. Back on the ground, he hopped out of the cockpit and walked slowly across the runway. At first he felt a little tired from his long struggle with Two-Face. But then the Batmobile caught his eye and he had a sudden burst of energy. A grin spread across his face.

Robin picked up his pace and dashed over to the Batmobile's driver-side door. He swung it open and hopped behind the wheel. Then he activated the communication device on the vehicle's instrument panel and spoke to his partner.

"Thanks for sending the Batmobile here on auto-drive as a decoy to fool Two-Face," Robin said. Then he asked hopefully: "Can I drive it back to the Batcave?"

"You've saved innocent people, thwarted several major crimes, helped capture a dangerous criminal and landed a biplane," Batman replied. "Make yourself comfortable in the driver's seat."

"Sweet!" Robin exclaimed as he grabbed the steering wheel.

"Now sit back and relax. The auto-drive will get you home," Batman said.

"Aww, man!" Robin sighed as the car sped away from Goodwin Airfield.

# TWO-FACE

**REAL NAME:** Harvey Dent

**OCCUPATION:**
Professional criminal

**BASE:** Gotham City

**HEIGHT:** 1.82 m

**WEIGHT:** 82 kg

**EYES:** Blue

**HAIR:** Brown/grey

**ABILITIES:** Criminal
mastermind and expert
marksman

**HOBBIES:** Flipping coins,
collecting coins, dividing
things by duality

Once considered Gotham City's "White Knight", Harvey Dent waged his war on crime the traditional way – through the US court system as its best district attorney. He developed a reputation as a protector and jailed many of Gotham City's most dangerous criminals. Harvey had a temper, but he could normally control it – until an explosion scarred half of his face. Then his darker side took control. As Two-Face, Harvey has become a man of two minds, with each side constantly at war with the other.

- Two-Face is divided between good and evil, and either side can take control at any time. But when it comes to a difficult decision, he resorts to flipping his lucky coin to choose his course of action.

- Harvey has an obsession with twos because of his double personality. His crimes often involve pairs, or twins, and he always has a back-up plan in case one scheme fails.

- Before the explosion changed Harvey Dent into Two-Face, Bruce Wayne and Dent had been close friends. Bruce still hopes that Harvey's good side will one day retake control and return Gotham City's greatest district attorney to his original form.

# BIOGRAPHIES

**Laurie S. Sutton** has read comics since she was a child. She grew up to become an editor for Marvel, DC Comics, Starblaze and Tekno Comics. She has written *Adam Strange* for DC, *Star Trek: Voyager* for Marvel, plus *Star Trek: Deep Space Nine* and *Witch Hunter* for Malibu Comics. There are long boxes of comics in her wardrobe where there should be clothing and shoes. Laurie has lived all over the world, and currently resides in Florida, USA.

**Luciano Vecchio** was born in 1982 and currently lives in Buenos Aires, Argentina. With experience in illustration, animation and comics, his works have been published in the US, Spain, UK, France and Argentina. His credits include *Ben 10* (DC Comics), *Cruel Thing* (Norma), *Unseen Tribe* (Zuda Comics) and *Sentinels* (Drumfish Productions).

# GLOSSARY

**accelerate**  increase the speed of a moving object

**acrobat**  person who performs gymnastic acts that require great skill

**analyze**  examine something carefully in order to understand it

**asylum**  hospital for people who are mentally ill

**auction**  sale during which items are sold to the person who offers the most money

**diversion**  something that distracts you from something else

**doppelganger**  person who looks almost exactly like another person

**perimeter**  outer edge or boundary of an area

**prominent**  widely and popularly known; leading

**venom**  poisonous liquid produced by some animals

**violate**  break a rule or a law

# DISCUSSION QUESTIONS

**1.** Two-Face makes many of his decisions based on the flip of a coin. Think of a time when you flipped a coin to decide something important. How did you feel about the result of the coin flip?

**2.** Why doesn't Batman let Robin drive the Batmobile? Should he give the Boy Wonder a chance behind the wheel? Explain your answers.

**3.** Why is the number two a part of every crime Two-Face commits? Does this pattern make it easier or harder for Batman and Robin to capture him? Discuss your answers.

# WRITING PROMPTS

**1.** Two-Face uses a doppelganger, or look-alike, to make it seem like he is in two places at once. Write a short story where Batman and Robin use doppelgangers to capture a villain.

**2.** Batman and Robin use many gadgets from their Utility Belts to capture their foes. Imagine you had your own Utility Belt. List and describe the tools you would carry on it.

**3.** In Arkham Asylum, Batman and Robin encounter an inmate strapped to a hospital trolley while they battle Two-Face. Write a short story explaining which super-villain that was and how he got there.